# EARTHLINGS

## SPECIAL AI EDITION

By Phil Growick

Colour Paperback ISBN 978-1-80424-351-0
ePub ISBN 978-1-80424-352-7
PDF ISBN 978-1-80424-353-4

Published by MX Publishing
335 Princess Park Manor, Royal Drive,
London, N11 3GX
www.mxpublishing.co.uk

Cover design by Brian Belanger
Cover image by Matt Growick

For Matt, Kevin, Jamie, Eliana, Bennett, Greyson,
Matt, Elizabeth and Maiju.

Always Maiju

# Contents

**Content (continued)**

Contents (continued, again)

# PREFACE

If reading these stories forces you to stop and take a breather because they're driving you mad, please take into account what they did to me, the author they first drove mad by creating them.

This is a special edition of EARTHLINGS (yeah, yeah; that's what they all say). The original (well, I didn't copy it from anyone) version is just text and you, the reader, would have to use your imagination (you've got a great one, right?) to work out what the EARTHLINGS might look like. So we thought, for the more (choose an adjective) reader, we would use the same AI tool that created the (choose an adjective) cover of EARTHLINGS to have a go at the characters themselves. We weren't quite ready for what it spat out but we're sure you'll agree they are (choose an adjective).

*All images were created by Phil Growick and Matt Growick using AI.*

There are, approximately, eight billion people on Earth.

Some belong someplace else.

No one could pronounce Yan Zxerx's name.  Including Yan.  He couldn't even spell it.

He began signing his name 'Xzerx'. Or 'Xxerx'. Or 'Zerxz'. He had a problem.

Then, one night, while on the way home from his weekly meeting of  Xenophobic Local 698, he was hit by a Salvation Army tuba dropped from an incredible height, and was ferociously flattened.

Since that time, Yan, of course, has become the inspiration for millions of pancake lovers the world over. And his famous 'ZXERX CAKES' have been enjoyed for decades. You remember the slogan:  Don't be jerks, enjoy some ZXERX!

But Yan met his untimely death last year when a nearsighted griddle man tossed Yan on the stove, cooked him (sunny side up), and served him to a family of out-of-town agnostics.

The entire family was then stuffed (well, they were already stuffed from ingesting Yan) and now stands on public display at Coney Island's Americana Exhibit where it's the main attraction.

Except for the wooden leg Captain Ahab used to entice Floretta Sweet.

# SCRALUM HIGGSBY

Scralum Higgsby's friends considered him a real, live wire. Quite literally. Because he had tens of millions of volts of electricity coursing through his body.

He was quite the rage at Christmas time. He'd make Mary glow, Joseph burn, and Jesus blink on and off in red, white and blue (and nothing quite so stirs the soul, especially at Christmas as a patriotic Jesus).

But soon he forsook his life of pious lust and headed for the big city. And that's where he made his mint. Also his maid. But that, too, is a different story.

During the famous blackout of the Eastern Seaboard, Scralum hired himself out to Con Edison. He then plugged himself into the main controls and supplied enough power to light the entire East Coast for an hour-and-a-half.

He next tried to show off to Zelma Blitz by lighting the West Coast simultaneously; but hopelessly short-circuited himself.

No longer able to tackle tasks of any great import, he relegated his life to one of blissful uneventfulness.

Last heard from, he was supplying power for a cheap 'EAT AT JOE'S' type diner on Highway 3.

Such had the mighty fallen.

# STARTLING HENRY

A certain code of ethics prohibits me from imparting precisely what Startling Henry did to attract attention.

However, there is no power on Earth which can prevent you, the reader, from using your imagination.

Galaxy Molasses had her vogue during the big saucer flap back in the late '90s.

Single-handedly, she captured fourteen flying saucers and exhibited their pilots and crews to the public.

Martians, Venutians, Mercurians, Saturnians. All were displayed for simple amusement. And amusing they most certainly were.

Who could but help but chuckle as the polka-dotted Sartunians whose forte was intercourse utilizing all fourteen of their genitalia?

Who could but help smiling as the tiny, razor-nosed Mercurians merged with the voluptuous Venutians?

And who found it impossible to stifle a guffaw as the Martians sat savagely lashing themselves with their tongues and tails?

It seemed no one.

The most tame New Year's Eve party in history was held on December 31, 2014 at the home of Mr. & Mrs. Calibre Feigenblatt.

There was no drinking, no dancing, no kissing, no joyous song and even no Ryan Seacrest.

On January 1, 2015, Mr. & Mrs. Feigenblatt and their guests were found to have been dead for three days.

# CLYME STRADMAN

Clyme Stradman was the world's top mountain climber (not literally meaning that he only climbed the world's top mountain, or that he climbed only mountain tops, but rather that he stood at the top of his profession; not literally meaning that he physically stood there, or even sat or reclined or lay or kneeled or splayed there, but rather that he was regarded by colleagues and the world press, as the best at what he did, which was climbing any mountain; well, not just *any* mountain, after all, there had to be some minimum requirement before Clyme would even agree to climb, such as height.

For instance, if a mountain wasn't really a mountain but just a hill, Clyme wouldn't even give it a second glance; not that he gave it a first glance, it's just that hills were beneath him; not literally under him; but since he was usually perched atop some of the tallest mountains in the world, he looked down on hills; both literally and figuratively. Finally, finished.

However, Clyme's parents couldn't spell. But they could climb. Which is what they did for a living.

Clyme's father, the now immortal Klutz Stradman, took Clyme on his first climb when he was only three (Clyme, that is, not his father; because how could his father be three and have a son? But you probably knew that already; not that Klutz took Clyme for this first climb when he was only three, but that a three-year old couldn't have a son).

You probably remember what happened to Klutz. It was in all the papers - when Clyme's mother, the now immortal Oops Stradman took Clyme on his second climb. You probably remember that one, too.

Oh, well. Clyme was on his own now (he tried to be on someone else's, but she kicked him off).

Soon, though, he was a full grown man anxiously awaiting his famous climb up the treacherously tall Mt. Blap, the graveyard of dozens of famous climbers (well, not literally their graveyard; no one came to lay flowers down, nobody cut the snow, there weren't any headstones or anything, it's just an expression; you know that. Hopefully).

Gathering together guides, food, and wooly mittens with Snoopy on them, Clyme fell in love with Bloomsie Yech (although that expression "fell" is not particularly appreciated by someone in Clyme's line of work). However, she repulsed Clyme's advances because Clyme repulsed her (he usually gave off the distinct aroma of a yak in heat).

Be that as it may, or June, the trek began.

Up and up they went; into the clouds. Beyond the clouds. Into the sky. Beyond the sky. Then they noticed that they'd passed the mountain. Not very many noticed in time. Fortunately for Clyme, he was the only one who did; he and Felicia Belch.

So, stranded top Mt. Blap, Clyme and Felicia made love to keep warm. They made love to keep cold. To celebrate Ground Hog Day. To commemorate Iwo Jima. That's all they ever did during those four horrible months. And help never came. Or went.

So Clyme, being a realistic son-of-a-gun, drew straws with Felicia (where he got the straws atop a mountain is not our concern), took whatever provisions they had left, left her stranded, and started on his way down.

Unfortunately, there seemed to be a little of Klutz and Oops in Clyme and he went  hurtling headlong towards earth at a tremendous speed (which, of course, you probably surmised since no one hurtles headlong towards earth at untremendous speeds).

Fortunately, his jacket opened, acted like a parachute and Clyme landed gently atop the Eiffel Tower where he was shot by Emmanuel Macron who was aiming at the current Duke of Wellington.

Tilly, better known to history as "The Scourge of the Desert Sands", spent her early life helping her father in the Filton Fush Market.

After his untimely demise (he was flattened by a frozen flounder), Tilly labored under a misapprehension, then an apprehension, then a seamstress. But her career was cut short when she accidentally sewed her thumb to a dress being shipped to a woman in Little Stink, Michigan (the woman received the dress, and the thumb, returned the dress but the thumb holds a most prominent place on her mantle, along with an amusing explanation she had printed and mounted on a thick cardboard).

So Tilly decided to strike it rich in another land. She booked passage to Crapistan where she set up a used camel business (preferred customers got two humps).

She also trapped anti-semitic Crapistanis, forcing them to gorge themselves on bagels, lox and cream cheese and to watch old Sarah Silverman videos.

Tilly was recently given a special award for her work in this field and had a forest planted in her honor in the same field.

But since the forest was planted around Tilly, she hasn't been seen or heard from for the last ten years.*

*If the statements in this report seem contradictory, it's just that the legend of Tilly T. Tischbaum is so

shrouded in mystery that it is extremely difficult to sift.

# FEBRUARY

Contrary to popular belief, the greatest lover in history was not Don Juan, nor Casanova, nor Errol Flynn, but Le Marquis de Hoboken.

On February 30, 1597, Le Marquis entered a monastery to atone for his sins. He was welcomed warmly by the brothers who used their illuminating method of illustration to illuminate generations innumerable.

# EGBERT HELLO, SHEBA SVELTE

## AND THE TERRIBLE INVASION OF THE GUMZLBRKMSNS

The day was like another day. Night crashed down on the city and the sun shone brightly.

The city's top scientists (not literally meaning that were scientists who studied and perfected arcane theories governing the laws of rotations of tops) were called together (not literally that they were all phoned at the same time, but rather than they were individually contacted and brought together for a meeting; of course, not literally meaning that they were taken in unison to the meeting, but rather that they were, forget it) to explain this phenomenon.

Pooling decades of intense, scientific study, knowledge, logic and the most sophisticated computers that man (or woman) could devise, the scientists claimed that Phaeton had probably busted a wheel on his chariot and without the aid of a heavenly AAA, was temporarily stranded mid-sky, The scientists were promptly reassigned to kitchen duty at the San Diego Zoo.

However, all was not lost (all was not found, either). High atop Mt. Blap, the world famous Carpathian Carunthian Observatory (dedicated to the found memory of Carpathian Carunthian, the noted astroproctologist), sat Egbert Hello and his incredibly delectable fellow scientist, Sheba Svelte.

Eyes alert, telescope poised, Egbert scanned the skies. THERE!!! MY GOD!!! (or your god). THERE!!! What was that bright, shiny object headed straight for the center of town? Could it be? NO…but YES!!! YES!!! It was a bright shiny object headed straight for the center of town!!!

Having just enough time to call the police, Egbert grabbed Sheba (though she had already warned him to cut that out: ("you pinheaded, swine-faced fart") and headed straight for the center of town.

There, right in the center of town, people were already panicking, running this way and that, that way and this, to and fro, fro and to, getting thoroughly seasick.

Egbert grabbed a loudspeaker from a police car and tried to calm the situation:

"LISTEN TO ME!!! THERE IS NO NEED TO PANIC!!! THESE MAY BE FRIENDLY VISITORS. FROM ANOTHER PLANET. WITH POWERS AND ABILITIES FAR BEYOND THOSE OF MORTAL MEN!!!

Egbert was promptly arrested for a blatantly adolescent plagiarism and hauled off as the bright, shiny object became even brighter and shinier (it was later approached by a detergent company to be used in a commercial: "We got our flying saucer 20% brighter and shiner with FLEB"!)

Slowly, out emerged the dreaded Gumzilbrkmsns. And what terrifying creatures they were. Though small, they resembled multi-hued Godzillas (how come there were never any Goddesszillas?).

They grabbed Sheba, re-entered their spacecraft and departed as quickly and quietly as they had come (they turned down the detergent offer; it seems that on their planet, they like to get things 20% darker and dingier).

To this day, the Gumzlbrkmsns, and Sheba, have not been seen or heard from.

But wait; up there! What's that bright, shiny object headed straight for the center of town?

# BLURKS FINCHEE

Blurks Finchee was an amazingly wealthy man.

He owned New York, Old York, Yorkshire pudding and Mt. Blap.

Blurks made his mint in the early days of Hollywood when he played romantic leads in such epic swashbucklers as "Crime And Punishment And Malteds".

But off screen, Blurks couldn't cut the mustard (come Thanksgiving he couldn't even cut the turkey).

Then, his mother, Sarah Finchee (you remember her, Miss Necrophilia of 1912), decided Blurks needed female companionship. So she introduced him to Martha Munch.

Perhaps a silly faux pas because Martha was a notorious glutton who soon ate Blurks out of house and home; then homes and gardens, then Reader's Digest.

Standing high atop Mt. Blap, Blurks thought of throwing himself into those tumultuous, churning waves below, but then a vision arose from the depths, a vision of Mother Mary; mother of Ralph who used to live down the block, and she told Blurks not to jump. So he didn't, because Blurks thought she was Mary, mother of Tony, who lived up the block and who was worshipped and adored by all the people up-block, down-block and mid-block.

On his way down, though, he was run over by a garbage truck.

Martha rushed to his side and disposed of the garbage.

Elmer was a nice sort of guy. Not tall, not short, just right. He wasn't fat, wasn't thin, just right.

And he wanted to marry his gloves.

Every night, Elmer would saunter up the winding stairway to his attic where the gloves lived, and hope for the best.

In his hand, tightly clasped, would be a bouquet of the sweetest smelling blossoms, blossoms purchased with his hard-earned pennies (he sold matches in the snow and business was faltering since he lived in Miami) from Yetta Futzer's Flower Boutique on the corner of Mondle and Kvetch.

Every night he repeated this ritual. And every night, when he'd proposed to his gloves, they'd just lie there without responding. Which gave him hope. Also Crosby.

Then it happened.

One night Elmer burst in upon his gloves making passionate love to his galoshes. It was too much for any man to endure.

Poor Elmer. If he'd taken the time to get better acquainted with his gloves, he'd have found that they were foot fetishists.

Elmer pondered this ironic twist of fate and came to the conclusion that fate was twisted. So he snuck back up to the attic, grabbed his gloves leaving the galoshes languishing behind.

A massive manhunt is on right now, so if you see a massive man, please report him.

To set the record straight, Brutus, Cassius, Casca, et.al., did not do their infamous deed on the Ides of March.

No. It was the Tides of March.

You see, two weeks previously, Caesar had been touting "Tides", the AMAZING, new toga detergent.

However, upon use, it left the togas tarnished.

In the Forum, as the senators attacked, Caesar had a violent reaction to Brutus' cologne and began sneezing uncontrollably.

His true famous last words were:  "AH CHOO, BRUTUS!"

Boss Nilch controlled the biggest political machine in Thwarp, Kentucky. But since there were only fourteen people in Thwarp (four of those being too young to vote, three being illiterate, and four who were "tetched" – the other three could not be found, though no one really tried very hard), Boss Nilch didn't control a very big machine.

But Boss Nilch had guts. No brains, heart, kidneys, liver or pancreas, just guts. Why many's the time you'd hear people say: "There goes Boss Nilch.  By gosh that guy's got guts!"

So Boss Nilch decided he'd like to make like a tree and branch out by becoming a state politician. Gathering the backing (and the fronting) of his neighbors, Ida and Zeke Flakefoot (soon to be parents of Crazy Luke Flakefoot), he set out for the big city.

Once in the big city, he set about opening headquarters. But flat broke, he had to settle for headpennies.

Now he was moving (not literally that he was moving things like furniture, but rather that he was in motion). He made a name for himself by championing the cause of The Tennessee Tartars,  a group of barbarians who raided and looted nearby towns, led by their leader (who else would they be led by, their follower?), Genghis Cohen.

Business looked up (it tried to look down but got vertigo). He opened a big, beautiful headhalfdollars and ran against the governor, Dwerm Gas (the only governor of the fifty states with one foot in the grave —well, he was a grave digger, after all). Boss Nilch won handily (but he didn't want to win handily, he wanted to be governor).

Egregiously heavy now, and loaded with riches, Nilch cast devious eyes at the White House.

Gathering together state support, (he got a hernia in the last campaign while mud wrestling with Irma Lard), he entered the primaries and soundly squelched his opposition.

Then he got the nomination of his party (why shouldn't he – he paid for the caterers, the tent, the band?).

Mounting the rostrum (he usually only did that when no one was watching) he let into one of the most floridly meaningless orations in recent political history (a record surpassed only by well, you know who).

The people went wild. So did Boss Nilch. He began frothing at the mouth and his head spewed forth molten lava.

From his vantage point high atop Mt. Blap, Boss Nilch listened to the election returns. His name was mentioned once or twice, but he'd lost the election by the largest margin in American history. It seems that he was just another fad, like the hula hoop; twirled around then tossed into the toy bin of tots.

Now, beaten and rejected, he tried in vain to regain his governorship, but lost the rudder. He was defeated by a fourteen –year-old salamander.

Hopping the first freight car back to Thwarp, he arrived in town amidst the huzzahs and cheers of the townsfolk. But they weren't for him; it seems that Crazy Luke was coupling with Pig Puss Polly in the town square.

Completely destroyed, Boss Nilch wandered out into the middle of the street where he was promptly run over by a garbage truck.

The townspeople, momentarily torn from Crazy Luke's fun time diversion, turned and said (those that were able): "There goes Boss Nilch. By gosh that guy's got guts!"

# SMOKEY COUPON

As a child, Smokey reveled in pulling the wings from the bodies of fallen angels; and in his innocent imaginings of furless, female raccoons as racy magazine centerfolds.

His adult life, however, was spent in more worthwhile pursuits.

On March 1, 1943, Smokey hijacked a busload of novices and led them into the tiny town of Temptation, Tennessee. To this day, not one has found her way out.

On January 29, 1954, Smokey forced an entire Hadassah mahjong meeting to sit for twenty minutes without say a word. Every member of that ill-fated meeting perished.

On October 25, 1959, Smokey invaded the sanctity of a confessional and sacrilegiously used a tape recorded to garner a best seller.

On November 3, 1964, he flicked cigarette ashes into a cremation urn, thereby mixing Michael Magee with a mentholated Marlboro.

On August 15, 1967, Smokey was run over by a garbage truck.

They think.

# TUGGLEBOAT, BABY

"Hiya, Tuggleboat!"

"Hiya, baby!"

"Whatddayadoin?"

"I dunno."

"Ya wanna do somtin?"

"I dunno."

"Whaddayadoin?"

"I dunno."

"Oh."

"Yeah."

"Ya wanna do somtin?"

"Aaaaahhh…"

"Yeah."

"Yeah, man. Taketeasy."

"Yeah."

"Yeah."

The world's perfect fool was the court jester for Henry VIII. His name was Giulo Guiseppi. From Naples. Born, and shedding his mortal coil, on April 1.

Unlike other jesters who'd gesticulate wildly or go through incredible gymnastics to make their masters laugh, Giulo would laugh himself.

But not just laugh. He would laugh violently and uncontrollably till Henry, Anne Boleyn and the entire court would, themselves, be laughing hysterically.

Unfortunately, on April 1, 1533, Giulo could not stop his heavy hysterics and after exploding his appendix, liver and Isles of Langerhans, he died.

However, several physicians swore that even after they certified him dead as the proverbial door nail, he continued to laugh. Furthermore, even after his deep internment, passersby claimed to hear that laughter emanating loudly from below.

# GILLY MOTHS

With wide-spread wings, evilly spotted black, Gilly Moths flitted about the flame.

The flame flitted back.

Gilly's heart pounded harder and harder.

The flame got brighter and brighter.

Gilly got closer and closer.

The flame got hotter and hotter.

Gilly got hotter and hotter.

The flame exploded.

Gilly exploded.

Sybelle Stutter, who had been calmly watching the doings while knitting a needlepoint depicting the fall of the Roman Empire, released excess gas.

Gracious Fred was more of a goodness than a gracious, for Gracious Fred was a man of the cloth. Not a priest. A tailor.

And whenever he handed his bill to his customers, they would exclaim in unmitigated disbelief: "Goodness gracious Fred, are you mad?"

The general consensus seemed positive.

Fred would sit stooped over a gray garment, incanting darkly to himself. Or press a pair of pants while calling up the wrath of Beelzebub upon unpaid customers.

Then, one night, just about midnight, while busily sewing Mr. Flatfoot's fly (it had been severed by an overanxious escort), Fred smelled something putrid. At first, he thought it was Mr. Flatfoot's fly. But when the Devil popped out of the dry leaning machine, Fred knew it had nothing to do with poor Mr. Flatfoot's fun time diversions.

"Gracious Fred?" asked the Devil.

"You got him", replied Fred.

"You bet your bottom, I do!" lascivioused the Devil.

But since Fred never did like having his bottom bet, nor his top, he kicked the Devil in his clove and went back to Mr. Flatfoot's fly.

Shortly, a near-sighted spider alighted atop said fly and began merrily chewing away.

In  the morning, when Mr. Flatfoot arrived to retrieve his trousers, all he found was a very fat, very incoherent spider, incanting darkly to himself.

# ALFRED HITCHPENIS

Unlike his more famous British cousin, *our* Alfred eschewed the crass and base vulgarization of his proper, Puritan surname and kept *his* in its truest, untouched form.

Unfortunately, it was the more popular, slang version of his name that gained prominence. Some say because his cousin was infinitely more talented. Or, some others say, because people just like to wallow in filth by saying his cousin's name. Or get a gleeful thrill out of continuously uttering foul language under the guise of pretentious intellectualism.

But be that as it may, at an early age Alfred exhibited an astonishing propensity with the motion picture camera and an amazing ability for pointing it in astoundingly inappropriate directions; almost always at the most astoundingly inappropriate of times (one need only to ask  his father and sensuous succession of nannies about that).

Now while it is true that his cousin Alfred almost always released his films ahead of *our* Alfred, it wasn't by much and, unfortunately, almost always with a title that seemed just one step ahead of poor Hitchpenis. As examples, a sample filmography follows of both auteurs:

| **HITCHCOCK** | **HITCHPENIS** |
| --- | --- |
| North By Northwest | South By Southeast |
| Rear Window | Rear Door |
| The Man Who Knew | The Man Who Knew |
| Too Much | A Little |
| Strangers On A Train | Strangers On A Bus |
| Vertigo | Scared of Heights |
| The Birds | The Parakeets |
| Lifeboat | Rowboat |

And perhaps his most famous, or infamous movie, depending on how you look at it, (or if you look at it), WACKO.

As you see, he was doomed to trail his cousin and without a doubt, he most certainly could never have appeared on television with the strict censorship of the time For which networks would have aired, at family time: The Alfred Hitchpenis Hour?

And though his cousin never won an Academy Award, this was small recompense to our Alfred. Consumed with jealousy and addled with rage, he stalked his cousin, brandishing 35mm movie reels which he tossed at his cousin's head, Frisbee style.

He continuously missed.

# JILBERT FRENS

Jilbert Frens loved to make friends.

He made friends with trees, rocks, ocean liners, king crabs, radiators, park benches, elevators, shoes, underwear, rugs, raccoon placentas and sun glasses.

But Jilbert was quite unpopular with people.

This didn't phase Jilbert. On the contrary, or off the contrary, he now went forward to make friends with bowl disinfectants, basketballs, snuff boxes, cuff links, charcoal, the sun, and match sticks.

Yet popular opinion was still against him.

Determined more than ever now to further his social position, he made friends with Forest Lawn Cemetery, curtain rods, poison ivy, linoleum, Egyptian cotton sheets, four-letter words and Jimmy Fallon's pancreas.

Still shunned as an outcast, Jilbert decided to hate a little.

He began to hate book ends, watch bands, sundials, ties, bridles, clothes pins and xylophones.

Rejected more than ever, he swore a life of revenge and sought it on paper clips, automobile mufflers, tinker toys, gravel, chopsticks and Pola Negri.

The world, shocked at this orgy of hate, demanded an apology from Jilbert.

He refused.

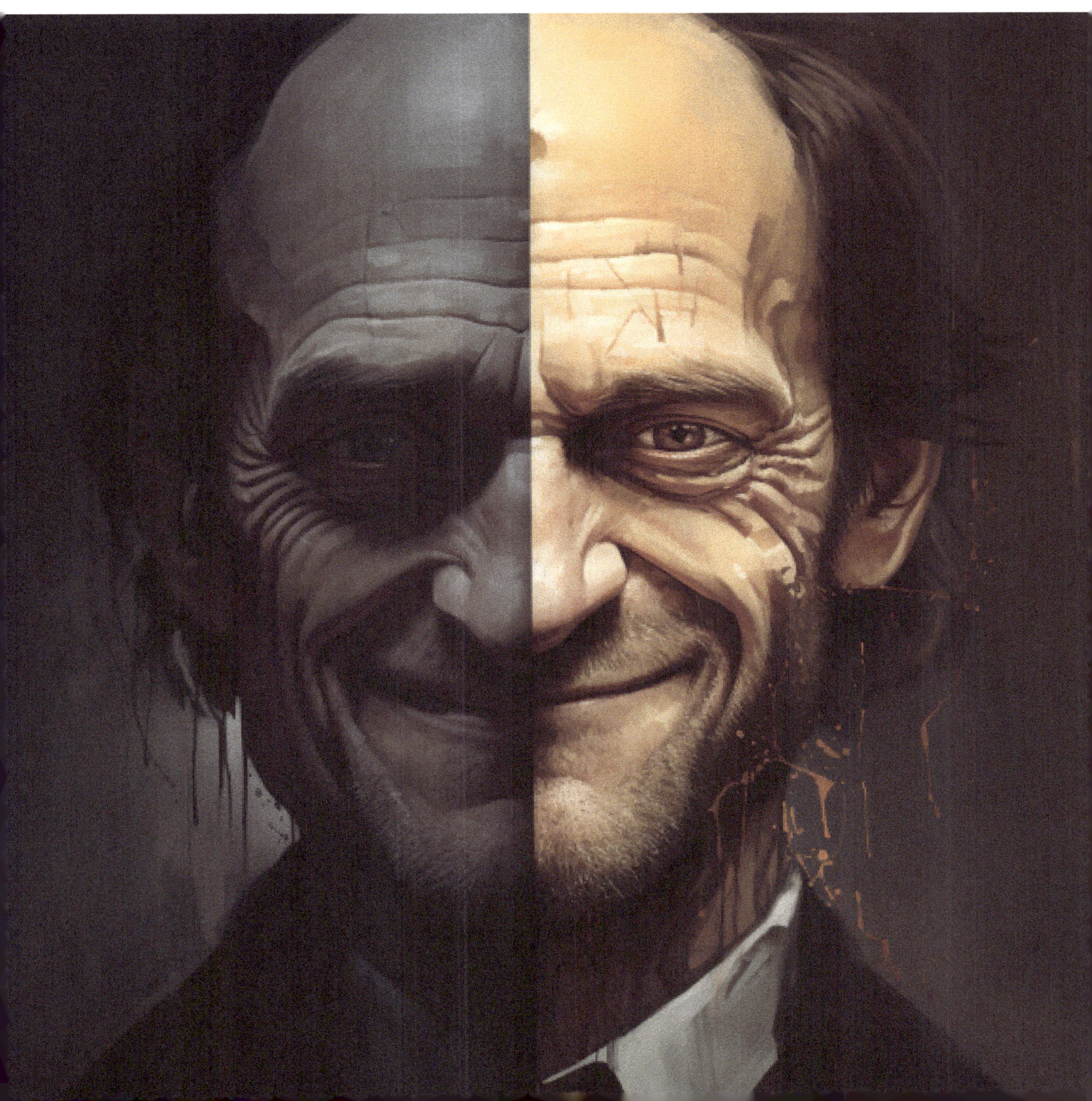

So on the night of December 25, Jilbert Frens had his feet pre-sweetened and was tickled to death by the furiously licking tongues of fourteen thousand, sugar-crazed puppies.

His was a truly sad case.

Sindgey Bop was a wild musician. Not a good one, just a wild one. So wild, in fact, that Sindgey was known to friends and foes alike as "that sonofabitch devil".

He even had a tail and horns. That's how he became a musician. He cut off his tail, kept his horns, stuck his fingers into his mouth and blew his brains out.

He was quite the novelty.

From miles around people would come just to see Sindgey blow out his brains. And the show he gave was truly sensational.

Smoke would stream from his horns. His face would turn fire engine red. And his nose would blink on and off quite violently. Soon, though, the strain began to show.

Informed by doctors that his madding pace would permanently damage his brain, Sindgey ignored their impassioned pleas (mainly for payment) and blew on to his heart's content; thereby bypassing his brain.

Then, one night in Little Stick, Michigan, it happened.

He tried to hit a high C and his nose fell off. Then his tongue fell out. His ears thudded to the floor. His hair broke into little pieces. His teeth plummeted to his toes. His eyebrows burned to a crisp.

His eyes rolled badly about (first in his head, then along the ground as happy, little children scrambled after them). And his head spewed forth lava.

The prediction had come to pass.

Sindgey's remains, if you're so inclined to look, lie in The Museum of Unnatural History. Visiting hours are all day Ferbsday until 6:73 and half-a-day Grunsday till 2:64.

Thank you.

# MAY

The largest flower ever grown was a Venus flytrap, nurtured by Mrs. Flora Stench of Partisan, Florida.

It was twenty-five feet high and weighed two hundred-forty seven pounds.

After winning first prize in the multi-continent, ultra-prestigious Flower Power Botanical Contest, Flora took her Venus flytrap home for feeding and was never seen again.

# MARCELA FRUNK

Marcela Frunk lived in a trunk. A fact in itself not extraordinary (an entire family had once resided in a shoe, and more than one show business personality claimed birth in a trunk); but this trunk belonged to a rather large and ferocious elephant.

Marcela wouldn't have it any other way. The elephant would.

So one day, gorged on peanuts, animal crackers and some Ex-Lax that the kind people had fed him, the elephant (really a poodle travelling incognito for the CIA in conjunction with MI6) dislodged Frunk from his trunk. Frunk, who was in her nightgown at the time, packed her bags and left her trunk with her trunk in her trunks.

Marcela protested this shabby treatment but go fight with an elephant once his mind's made up.

So Marcela began her now famous journey to East Petunia, Iowa the flower of the Ozarks.

Once in town, she created an immediate and wildly enthusiastic sensation, The local hillbillies, none of whom had even seen shoes before, took Marcela for a "dern freak" who could take off her feet.

From miles around, people would come and pay five cents to see the "city gal" with the podiatry puzzle.

Then, after twelve years of booming business, Marcela met and married Willow.

Willow was a young, beautiful hilly billy. But she'd weep at the slightest provocation. The townspeople even named a tree after Willow:  Crybaby.

The two remain happily married to this day and Marcela, (who had bought three pairs of tiny mittens), bills her children as being able to take off their hands.

Wily mother.

Sal's problem was keeping up with Joneses.

Everything they had was bigger. Their house. Their bankroll. Their mouths.

But it was their daughter, Luscious, who Salvatore really coveted. She was aptly named. She was majestic. Flawless. Lindsey Vonn could ski between her breasts. And Luscious became an obsession with Sal. Also with anyone else who saw her.

Having coveted his neighbor's goods (who covets their neighbor's bads?), Sal did a bit of soul searching. However, the Josiah Tabernacle Choir did not appreciate their soul being searched, so he gave up the search, and had to give up on Luscious, as well.

Salvatore, knowing now that he could never have Luscious and stay in the church, turned himself over to gay abandon. And gay abandon turned him over to his brother, Reckless.

The final loss of Luscious drove poor Salvatore mad. Like a mad cow. However he couldn't supply any milk (pasteurized or skim) and there's been no change in his condition since.

It is said that if you're driving through the countryside on a pitch dark night, if you listen intently, you can hear Salvatore mooing plaintively.

Or could it be Luscious, longing for the love she so callously abjured?

# STERLING MONEY

Having been born into the richest family on earth, Sterling Money surprised friends and foes and family alike by renouncing his incalculable wealth (he had tried to calc but ignominiously gave up when his savings alone surpassed the cumulative American deficit to the year 2069), and entering a convent.

He also surprised the resident Mother Superior, who, in her youth, had been *that* "Bubbles O'Toole". And being *that* "Bubbles O'Toole, she understood Sterling's need for anonymity and permitted him in under the strictest secrecy, or sacristy, I forget which.

Concealing his identity beneath a novice's habit (luckily for him the novice had a habit of harboring various and sundry in her habit), he remained in the convent and became a full-fledged sister: Sister Mary Margaret Monahan Murphy.

Society was shocked to learn of his impending divorce from Jesus on the grounds of incompatibility.

# JUNE

The biggest wedding in history was held on June 23, 1993 by Mr. & Mrs. Irving Schmutz, for their twenty-nine year-old daughter, Yetta.

It cost $13,890,763.14 and accommodated 9,140 guests.

It was also the first time in history that everyone who was invited attended.

Except the groom.

# PUGNACIOUS BOB

Pugnacious Bob was a prize fighter. Everywhere he went, he fought with prizes.

In Oklahoma, he had a monumental match with a ten-foot tall oak door (it was a door prize), but lost when he was hit in the eye with a knob (not the door's, Gloria Tweedy's).

In Illinois, he won a three-round decision over a $250 combination color TV and FM/AM stereo radio (some claimed the fight and he TV, were fixed, but considering the expertise of TV repairmen, highly unlikely).

In Seattle, he battled to a draw against a Grecian urn (after the fight the urn went to pieces).

In Phoenix, he lost an eleven-round bout to an electric hair dryer when he was hit below the belt (the pug's plug still bothers him).

But in New York he made up for his defeats during a 400 round match that pitted Bob's strength, stamina and skill against the incomparable ease and handling of a church raffle Cadillac.

He recently retired from prize fighting, but has remained an active campaigner against church bazaars and Hadassah mah-jongg tournaments; actions which have caused him to excommunicated on one hand and involuntarily circumcised on the other.

# MANGUS FLOBORE

Nothing was the matter with Mangus, but he thought there was.

He as the world's foremost hypochondriac (he had tried to be fivemost, but fore was the most).

It all began when Mangus was just six months old. His mother, the new immortal (and immoral) Curmudgeon Flobore, dropped him on his head.

For days Mangus lay in a tizzy. But Tizzy didn't like being layed in, so she unceremoniously made him vacate her premises. In fact, after that, Mangue could never keep a premise.

Then he met Peshka.

Peshka was a round-shouldered beauty, not unreasonably resembling Quasimodo.

It was love at first sight.

An improvement immediately swept over Mangus. But it kicked up too much dust and he began sneezing ceaselessly.

After a while, Peshka couldn't take it anymore. She cut off Mangus' nose. It stopped the sneezing, but it clogged up his ears.

Be that as it may, the two were amazingly happy. During intercourse, they would make the most of Peshka's Quasimodo resemblance and ring bells after each climax.

It was a novel innovation in sex and it soon touched off a national craze for what the French called "La Belle Quasimodo". It brought an astounding uptick in business at bell stores and Notre Dame but had nothing to do with the fire. It is said.

But Mangus soon became involved with Sasha Twirl on the sly, When on the sly proved uncomfortable, they moved to the settee. And had the misfortune of being trapped in a convertible sofa.

Mangus was never the same after that.

Shortly, he died.

So did Peshka.

No word on Sasha.

Who cares?

# FIVES KRAP

Fives was a concert pianist.

He was the toast of Europe and the English muffin of America. Women flocked to him in droves. Also in cars. Especially women who drove cars.

But Fives preferred biting his nails. On his toes.

For hours he'd sit, hunched up on the floor, nibbling away. He neglected his piano, his practicing, his women, practicing with his women. All because of this carefree penchant for toenail biting.

Then, one fateful day, it happened. While hunched and nibbling, Fives was frightened by a bible salesman; but he couldn't remember if it was an old New Testament salesman, or a new Old Testament salesman, or a new New Testament salesman or an old Old Testament salesman.

Be that as it may, Fives bit off nine toes.

He took to the streets, but the streets didn't take to him, so he took to the gutters. And when the gutters didn't want him he took to the leaders. Here, he found peace and tranquility (a down and out Las Vegas lounge act).

Fives moved beneath the city streets and you can still hear stories of people claiming to hear impassioned piano playing coming up from the bowels of the city.

But only when Fives eats chili.

# JULY

The largest firecracker in history was built by The Acme Gunpowder Company of Dismal, Arkansas, in 1879.

It weighed forty-three thousand tons, stood fifty-eight stories high, and was set to go off on the evening of July 4 during the annual Independence Day celebration.

On the evening of July 3, however, Mr. Selmer Kiak, the firm's night watchman, accidentally ignited the fuse while trying to singe the whiskers of a pesky yeti.

Immediately, The Acme Gunpowder Company went out of business.

As did the entire state of Arkansas.

CE
CIE CIE
CIE CIE

Blaggart was a braggart. And whenever people talked about his big mouth, they really knew what they were talking about.

For his mouth, through some genetic oversight, extended from the top of his nose to the bottom of his Adam's apple. And whenever he laughed, his Adam's apple would bob up and down and knock out his teeth.

So Blaggart tried not to laugh. And because he didn't laugh, he became unhappy. And because he became unhappy, he became a monster.

Every night, when the clock struck twelve, his face would immediately be covered with thick, black hair, his incisors would extend to become long, glisteningly white fangs, his nails on his fingers and toes would grow inches and culminate in an amazing point, and foam would flow freely from his mouth.

But at exactly 12:01, he remedied the situation by:

1. Going to a barber

2. Going to a dentist

3. Going to a manicurist

4. Going to pot

From pot, he went to euphoria and from there he didn't care where he went.

But the cops did.  That's why they busted him.

Born in Little Stink Michigan, Aaron's early life was spent in total obscurity. Then at the age of twenty-three, he suddenly applied for patents on the telephone, telegraph, ear wax, kosher delicatessens, Scarlett Johansson and "Captain Billy's Whiz Bang".

He spent the next twenty-three years in the Little Stink State Penitentiary.

There, he applied for patents on telescopes, the Roman Empire, false teeth, Wendell Willkie's nose, and "Smokey the Bear".

Upon his release in 1941, he joined the Marines and spent time fighting in Inner and Outer South Pago Pago.

Elated by his applications for patents on the aircraft carrier, Hedy Lamar and Harry Truman, he fought through jungle and swamp till his capture by the Japanese.

While in a POW camp, he applied for patents on bubble gum, jockey shorts, Jane Russell, watch bands, John Philip Sousa, tulips and cucumbers.

Upon his return to Little Stink, he was hailed as a hero, given the Medal of Honor and run over by a garbage truck.

Posthumously, he was denied patents on 1946, kidney stones, belly button lint, picture frames, Napoleon's knees, waxy buildup and Utah.

Fran loved to talk. And she especially loved to talk on her EYEPHONE.

In fact, she was the first one to own an EYEPHONE. Because the operation to install one into one's eye socket was prohibitively expensive.

When the EYEPHON was first introduced, critics, mostly, castigated the creators for such a biological intrusion. "Frankenstein redux", they screamed. Ophthalmologists clucked and brandished outsize eye charts.  Retinologists scratched their heads and babbled incoherently. And plastic surgeons sharpened their scalpels and had a field day.

Once the EYEPHONE was surgically placed on one's head, yes, that person would be able to talk and see who they were talking to, but the EYEPHONE was large and gave one the appearance of a slobbering cyclops. And if not properly installed, when one would look down, the EYEPHONE had a disconcerting habit of falling into one's vichyssoise.

However, since Fran was the first person to sport the EYEPHONE in public, she was hired by an ad agency to appear in the launch campaign.  Remember "I've got my eye, and EYEPHONE, on you, baby."?

But then Fran outdid herself and had a second EYEPHONE implanted; in the other eye. This gave her the startling ability to talk to two people at the same time and see them simultaneously. It was 2D (D for dementia).

However, her eyes became permanently crossed and she was run over by a garbage truck because she wasn't sure in which direction she was going.

The longest vacation in history was taken by the McSquiggle family of Pine Tar, Oregon.

They left their home headed to the vast Oregon forests on August 12, 2004 and didn't return till August 12, 2005.

Since none in the family had applied for anything longer than two weeks, their family members, employers and the police, demanded to know where they were for a full year.

Bertram McSquiggle claimed the family had been kidnapped by aliens and brought to the aliens' home planet of Xcvpryz. Not only that, but Kate McSquiggle had been mated with an alien and to prove it showed everyone little Brsfqnxz.

When no one believed their story, Kate emitted a loud and ear-splitting sound calling an intense beam of light to envelope the group and whisk them all up to Xcvpryz.

Now let's see how they explain *that* when their next vacation is due.

Back in the wild and wooly west, where men were men and women were woolier, one name stands out bigger, taller, huger, and more cursed than all the rest: "Wild Bill" Dingleberry.

"Wild Bill" (he got the name after one of his more infamous orgies, when request for payment was made by the local Madame and he replied: "Gawsh, that wuz some wild partee! But gawsh, this here's some wild bill!"

Yes, Bill was the Old West's most notorious turncoat and low-down-ornery polecat.

He was driven out of every town he ever entered (and why not, he paid his chauffeur good money), and was despised by every decent, law-abidin' Christian in the territory (this did not take into account Native American beliefs nor any Orthodox Hasidim who happened along).

But that didn't bother Bill. Nosireebob!

He sold more guns to the Indians, whiskey to the white folk, guns to the white folk, whiskey to the Indians and got very confused in the process.

But the law was closin' in.

President Rutherford B. Hayes sent out his most secret agent to bring in Bill alive or dead. With the emphasis on the doornail.

The agent was the immortal Buck Tooth.

Buck caught up with Bill in the sleepy, little town of Zzzzzz, Arizzzona and the two proceeded to shoot it out.

Unfortunately for Bill, he proceeded to get shot up. But he had it comin', that no-good-lily-livered-yellow-bellied-sidewinder!

And Buck, the schmuck, was hailed as a hero.

He returned to Washington amidst the loud huzzahs of his countrymen (some city men, too). And President Hayes pinned a medal to his chest. But a bit too deep.

Buck is buried in Arlington National Cemetery, right next to Bill. It's only fitting, as people winsomely peruse Buck's epitaph:

He gave "Wild Bill" his belly fill,

But got kilt by a pin,

Tough on him.

# STANLEY

Born into the world at a time of grave national peril (Kevin Costner had just been shot off his horse), Stanley's parents took him home from the hospital and promptly forgot where they put him.

Left unattended for the next twelve years, Stanley made the most of it and grew up. His parents, walking into a broom closet by mistake, once again accepted him into the fold

But Stanley wanted to be accepted into the family. This though, was quire impossible. So for the time being, Stanley had to remain content with being the pride of the fold.

How he delighted in it.

From miles around the fold would come to welcome him into it.

"What a darling boy", they would say.

"What a darling girl", they would say.

"What a darling…"they would shrug as they drifted off into conjecture.

It was then that Stanley met Rosalinda. Rosalinda was a gorgeous hunk of monkey who put bananas away like there was no tomorrow. Stanley, entranced by her beauty proposed and they were married shortly thereafter.

The years sped by and Rosalinda, downing bananas at an alarming rate, grew to tremendous proportions. It was then that tragedy struck.

King Kong, grown nearsighted from a bad fall (spring and summer hadn't gone all that well, either), mistook Rosalinda for Fay Wray and ran off with her.

Stanley, destroyed financially from the long years of keeping Rosalinda in bananas, contemplated suicide. Then his navel.

Standing high atop Mt. Blap, he blew a farewell kiss to Rosalinda and plunged headlong into the furious waters below.

When they fished him out about a month later, they found this note pinned to his belly-button:

"Tell Rosalinda I love her even now.

  P.S. There's a fresh crate of bananas in the fridge."

From the distant corners of the world came the fold to his funeral. And as the last eulogies were being read, the chapel doors swung open and in swung Rosalinda.

Tears streaming down her cheeks, arms dragging along the floor, she shuffled over to Staley and placed one last, loving kiss on his lips.

And a frozen banana into his hands.

Moral:  Don't monkey with Stanley.

# IS BIG BIRD THE REINCARNATION OF

# ALEXANDER THE GREAT?

This is a very grave question that's been plaguing historical scholars and parapsychologists for decades.

But next year we'll know for sure. For next year, Big Bird will try to conquer Greece, Persia. Egypt and India.

If the quest succeeds, fine.

If not, not.

The longest Labor Day Party in history began on September 2, 1822 and ended on September 3, 1875.

There were hot dogs, cold cats, beer, casks of ale and free intelligence tests which proved beyond a doubt that had the IQ of most of the attendees been two points lower, they'd be classified as plants.

Many became United States Senators.

# SVERG P. LARTS

Sverg P. Larts was not Scandinavian, as his initial implies. Swerg was nothing. In fact, he was a man without a country. And this came about quite tragically.

When Sverg was sixteen he lived in Upper Euthanasia (Lower Euthanasia had recently been made a commonwealth of Upper Hydrophobia) where his father and mother were makers of shoes.

As a rule, Mrs. Larts was fond of loafers while Mr. Larts was very fond of sneakers. Since Sverg was fond of neither, they cast him into the ocean tied to a fourteen- ton weight.

Sverg sank immediately (no one takes their time sinking while tied to a fourteen-ton weight).

But, gnawing through the ropes at a remarkable rate (his front teeth were the size and sharpness of a glandular rabbit's), he quickly swam to the surface, bid an unfond adieu to his native shores and undauntingly began chugging out to sea.

About the fourth day out, his arms got tired. The fifth day, his legs got tired. By the sixth day, he sprouted gills, fins, scales and began his new incarnation as a dashing halibut about town.

By the seventh day he was engaged to be married to Sissy Nubile, a stunning, young mermaid who'd been around the pool once or twice already.

By the end of the fourth month, he became a teacher in a school of fish.

By the end of that week, he was floundering (which was horrible when you're married to a mermaid who was known to philander with a flounder).

Then he was caught in a tuna net and wound up as the roommate of Charlie.

That's why he has no country.

Here was a man! Here was a conqueror! Here was a nice, Jewish boy. Oy!

All his life, Genghis led others. It was inherent in his blood (that's why he was anemic; no room for hemoglobin).

And lead he did.

Who can forget Genghis riding down fiercely across the steppes of Moronia at the head of his fearless minions (you need at least ten men for a minion).

Who can forget all the monumental and historic battles he won (including the one with his mommy who made him wear earmuffs when he went conquering in the snow-he shouldn't get a cold).

And who can ever forget the huge empire he carved out of three continents (and let's not forget the Thanksgiving turkeys); the bagels and nova and cream cheese laid at his feet; the blintzes at his command; the drinking bouts where gallons of egg creams were consumed by his orgiastic troops?

No, Genghis is very hard to forget.

But let us try.

# TRILLS BOWNMAN AND JOAN FREEN

Trills Bowman was not quite a man He was not quite a woman. Trills Bowman was a carrot.

He lived, or rather grew up, in Farmer Grulls' garden; and he truly liked it. Why shouldn't he? He was engaged to be seeded with a delicious young tomato named Joan Freen. And when the other fruits and vegetables had their backs turned, Trills and Joan would wildly cross-pollinate.

But happiness is a short-lived luxury, and one day tragedy struck the love couple.

Farmer Grulls decided to enter Joan in a tomato contest, dug her up, roots and all, and no woman (or tomato), want their roots showing.

Trills, not to mention Joan (okay, I won't mention her) were quite upset. But Trills could do nothing. He just planted there, gaping sadly at Joan's exposed stem.

Into the big city went Joan and Grulls. She was placed on a cushion of purple, right next to a rather over-ripe grape going under the handle of Fernando Armpit. This foul demon kept proposing that the two run off together and make punch. Joan began to sob uncontrollably.

But Trills to the rescue.

He disguised himself as an anchovy and Minute, Grulls' son, dug him up as an entry in the pizza topping contest.

"JOAN! JOAN!" Trills called. Then he spotted her cowering next to that lecherous grape.

Trills dispatched him with one good stomp. Now he and Joan had to move fast.

Grabbing her by the stem, something she never let him do in public, Trills ran for the exit, Joan rolling happily behind.

Making their way through the tangle of the city, they beat it back to the farm where the sympathetic fruits and vegetables hid them from the vengeful wrath of an infuriated Farmer Grulls.

But time heals all wounds and Grulls finally gave his consent for the two love plants to be weeded and wedded.

What a beautiful wedding it was.

Peach, the apricot, administered the services, Olive, the olive, played the organ and sang, and soon the newlyweds ran off to their waiting seed-bed.

Both were delirious with joy until tragedy overtook them.

Ursula Stump, a rather aged rabbit left empty through loss of strategic fornication, decided that Trills would make a wonderful contribution to her eyesight. So she invaded the holy, nuptial privacy of the seed-bed and hopped away with Trills dangling limply between her two bunny teeth.

Joan was beside herself with grief. No more Trills. No more cross-pollination. But Trills, a virile, young carrot, had done his job well.

Nine months to the day of that awful tragedy, Joan gave seed to a happy, bouncing, four-ounce baby Carrato. The first of his kind.

Joan is quite happy today, for her son, Trills, Jr., has been selected by Birdseye as the newest, up and coming ubiquitous comestible.

Now Joan can join Trills, happy in the knowledge that their great love had not been in vine.

# OCTOBER

The most infamous witch in history, feared by everyone, everywhere, every Halloween, was Brunhilda Setchikaya. She lived in the tiny, tucked away hamlet of Batswing, Transylvania.

She was credited with casting over nineteen thousand spells (yet she flunked spelling in junior high) and with having turned fourteen princes into tadpoles.

She was especially fond of young, good-looking princes and loved to watch the tadpoles.

It is rumored that she served as a model for one of the witches in the opening of Macbeth, because she loved to shake spears, too.

# GLURG HERF

Glurg Herf was an incurable romantic. He'd make love to books, snails, keyboards, anything within reach.

It began when his mother Ptolemy Herf (you remember her, the 1903 Miss Chicago Stockyard), hit him on the head with his father (you remember him, the 1903 Mr. Chicago Stockyard).

When Glurg awoke, he immediately ran to romp and frolic with rest of the llamas. Yes, Glurg thought he was a llama (yet he didn't live in Peru nor anywhere near the Bronx Zoo).

But he was happy. And that's what counted. His calculator also counted, but that can be discounted here.

From miles around, little freckle-faced fantasists would come to feed him; and his parents welcomed these simple acts of kindness because they cut the cost of llama feed in half.

Yet as time rolled on, Glug did become unhappy. He detested his cage. So one day, as a buxom, buck-toothed, tooth-braced lass reached in to give Glurg a peanut, he pulled her to him, and though momentarily smothered in braces and breasts, forced his parents to unlock the cage.

Prancing merrily onto the street, he was soon gone.

For days, a nationwide manhunt ensued. But since Glurg was a llama, the search proved futile.

Presently, he came to rest in a deep, dark forest where he fell in love with an oak tree. The tree, quite immobile, refused Glurg's advances and heaped insults, and acorns, Upon his head.

Glurg, naturally disappointed, trudged off to Mt. Blap.

Today, as he rests stuffed upon his parents' fireplace, visitors come for one last, long, longing look at Glurg Herf, llama extraordinaire.

At two bucks a head.

Zilda Rich was exceedingly poor. Perhaps that's why she enthusiastically embraced the life of concert escort.

Besides mingling with the greats and near-greats of the philharmonic world, her monetary rewards were great, or near-great, depending on who she was mingling with.

Her early career brought her into the gilded boudoirs of such symphonic genii as Garbo Splitter and Sergio Malconentente.

Her later career brought a change of tune. For Zilda was growing old. Also warts. Also deaf. And no one, not even the excusably trisexual concert conductors, wanted any part of her. Literally and figuratively.

But Jimmy Strumpet did. All of her. And he got it. So did she. They deserved it.

# FATHER MOTHER AND MOTHER FATHER

In the beginning, there was Rupert.  Rupert Mother. Descended from a long line of Mothers.

And not far from the birthplace of Rupert Mother, was born Drusilla Father.

An explanation is necessary here. Rupert and Drusilla were members of a quirky Catholic sect which, unlike mainstream Catholic Diocese, mandated that their clergy maintain their last names for address, rather than using their first names.

So, when Rupert became a priest, he became Father Mother. And when Drusilla became a Mother Superior, she became Mother Father.

As to the location of this somewhat distinctive Catholic enclave, it spread across a small county in New Hampshire with similarly quirky names. Rupert was from Breakfast, New Hampshire, while Drusilla was from Lunch, New Hampshire.

So when mass was given, you were having Breakfast or Lunch.

And so it came to pass that Father Mother and Mother Father met one fateful day in the tiny hamlet between Breakfast and Lunch, Brunch, New Hampshire.

And as it happens so often within the Bible, Father Mother and Mother Father, though fighting their feelings, fell deeply in love and regretfully left the Church.

However, they lived happily ever after and their progeny did so, as well.

You may recall Brother Sister and Sister Brother.

# STEVIE SALAMANDER

How Stevie loved to hide under rocks. Or jump from leaf to leaf. Oh, what a ball she had (she kept it after a wild night of orgiastic reveling with gophers and crickets).

But Stevie's main claim to fame was her remarkable sense of humor, which she inherited from her grandfather, the now American institutionalized, Mosely Cracker.

And it was that uncanny sense of humor that catapulted Stevie into the glittering world of the theatre.

For almost fifty-two years, Stevie Salamander enchanted and captivated audiences with her hilariously amusing interpretation of a salamander dancing Swan Lake.

But as time went on, Stevie began to dry up. So booking passage with a herd of licentious locusts (some fresh from a ravenous run in Utah), she flew directly to Finland where she was brought to life once again with miraculous hormone shots.

Unluckily for Stevie, they were male hormones injected by a deranged doctor who considered himself a funny Finn and who called himself Huckleberry.

Now Stevie sought the safety of rocks, once again and was attacked by a territorial squirrel.

Stevie did not survive, but the squirrel was last seen continuing to store nuts.

# THE PORTRAIT OF DORIAN PLAID

Once upon a time in jolly old, merry old, rollicking old England, there was born one Dorian Plaid. Had there been born two Dorian Plaids, this would be a tale of twins, although it's doubtful that Mr. and Mrs. Plaid would've named both babies Dorian. One, of course would've been Dorian; the other conjecturally, Seymour; that is of course had the other not been a girl, in which case she may have been named Conchita (although there is no Latin blood in the Plaid lineage – that they know of).

Dorian grew up handsome and tall, slender and wise, filthy and corrupt. What joy he was to his parents who heaped upon him all the advantages: money, wealth, riches, Amex Platinum.

Yet these advantages did nothing to sully young Dorian's character. But when Dorian's character (Blaze Bliss, and what a character she was ) was kicked out of the house, they did much to sully Dorian.

Take women. He did. From here and there they would flock to his side, and his side was usually along with the rest of him in bed. No, Dorian suffered not from sex (oh, well, maybe that one time when that rash gave him quite a start. His doctor told him he had non-specific urethritis and Dorian asked if he could be more specific. He couldn't).

Then it happened. He sat for a portrait by the Devil. And the Devil used oils because watercolors evaporate in his neck of the woods.

Now up and down the docks Dorian wandered. Slumming with the scum, trifling with the base creatures who haunted the bars.

Then, while trifling a bit too hard, his portrait turned to dust. Dorian followed suit. He also followed sweaters. And any lovely ensemble. Yes, Dorian Plaid had become quite the clothes horse (he even had horse shoes).

He would slink in the darkness, waiting for a lovely, young pair of jeans to go by and then make his move. But it wasn't only jeans he craved, he also dallied with blouses, scarves, vests, pantaloons. He wasn't picky. Except if a sweater had lint.

Oh, base creature. Dorian was a devil incarnate. Sunken to depths unknown to man (and a couple of women).

But with his portrait gone, Dorian continued to look youthful. For three hundred and sixteen years he looked like Bradley Cooper. But he was growing weary of making love to synthetics, so he called upon the Devil to release him from his ill-conceived pact. The Devil refused.

So on a dark, dank night, Dorian had another portrait painted, this time at Walmart, and he immediately wasted away. However his portrait is beautiful. And, if you wish, you can have lovely wallet size copies made for next to nothing.

# NOVEMBER

The largest Thanksgiving feast ever consumed by one human being consisted of twelve twenty-pound turkeys; eighteen cases of cranberry sauce; one hundred sweet potatoes; three creates of peas and carrots; two cauldrons of stuffing; fourteen gallons of ice cream; and nine jars of maraschino cherries.

It was eaten by Mr. Parliament Strugges of Calliope, New Zealand.

He was then severely chastised by his wife and sent to bed without any supper.

# SLEED SOD

Sleed Sod's head was attached to his navel. This presented a problem because he slept on his stomach. But other than that, he was socially accepted as quite the dashing fellow.

Having his head on his stomach had certain distinct advantages for Sleed: food had a much shorter trip to digestion, one pill would suffice for both headache or stomach ache, he could stand on his head and his body would become a seesaw, he could walk unafraid of being punched in the nose because his nose was below his belt, he could always stick his nose into everyone's business, he was hired at Bernum & Blowhard's as a happy attraction for the little kiddies.

It was here that Sleed met the love his of his life, Ethel Spupp.

Ethel wasn't a bearded lady as everyone thought. No, on the contrary, she was a ladied beard. And she and Sleed hit it off splendidly. When they'd make love, people would comment on the fine beard Sleed had, or how well off puberty had left him (depending on how they were making love).

Then tragedy struck.

One quiet day, as they made love in the grass, Ethel was cut down by a lawn mower.

Sleed, having nothing else to live for, decided to end it all right there.

So he did.

It was the end of one of the most famous love affairs in history.

Yes, this is *the* Hamps Bridgey, the one you've heard so much about.

Hamps' mother (the infamous escort "Toll" Bridgey) had an illicit affair (who has licit affairs?) with Hamps' father, George Washington Bridgey, and bore him a son. She also bored him to death. Which is where he went.

So "Toll" brought Hamps up all by herself, which took quite a toll on "Toll"; but she raised him to be a perfect gentleman. That way, he'd never hurt a girl the way his father had hurt her.

Unfortunately, from the moment of his birth, when he grabbed the attending nurse's booty, Hamps looked as though he would wear his father's shoes (which was very unhygienic because G.W., as his friends liked to call him, had athlete's feet (just where he got the athlete's feet, how he got them, who was the athlete, and why didn't he return the feet, still remains shrouded in mystery).

Hamps decided that marriage would cure him of his galloping satyriasis, and married Dr. Florence Plop, the noted hysterectomist. Then he married "Busty" McCoy, the noted "model". Then Clarabelle Wallop, the noted noter. Unfortunately he marred all three simultaneously, and, as penance, on the night of December 28, 1944, was forced to make love to a Calamity Jane look-alike.

# RAPUNSEL STRIPES

Rapunsel Stripes was a gorgeous, willowy, frisky young lass with twenty-five feet of flaming red hair. All on her eyebrows. Twelve-and-a-half feet on each side.

She didn't have any beaus, but she did have a lot of bows.

That's what she did with her hair. She made bows. Also arrows.

And she could truly hit the mark. Also the Tom, the Dick and the Harry. Which is why she didn't have many beaus. After all, who wants to date a woman suffering from the dreaded "William Tell Syndrome"?

After a night of dining and dancing, she would repair to her boudoir with her date, and there, permit him to take her only after shooting an apple off his head.

Needless to say, she didn't have many takers. In either sense of the word.

So Rapunsel decided to advertise on all social dating media, especially the "Apple Of My Eye" site.  She had a picture of her, bows on brows, with the words: Expert archer looking for right Adam's apple and arrow.

Amazingly, she was besieged with takers. In fact, she was taken so many times she became mistaken.  And so ended her penchant for archery. But even now, whenever she hears The William Tell Overture, she runs naked into the night looking for Robin Hood.

# DECEMBER

The longest snowball fight in history began on December 15, 1783 between two Finnish families.

It blossomed into a full-scale tribal war that ended suddenly on December 23, 1789.

Along with the two Finnish families.

Sir Reginal Bald was not his real name. His real name was a simple Reginald Bald; but when King Zephyr Nighted him (he often dayed him, too), Reginald Bald was now Sir Reginald Bald.

Sir Reginald had one frustrating feature that belied the name of Bald. He was just one unruly mass of hair (his parents had tried to remedy the problem with lawn mowers, weed killers and locusts; all to no avail).

However, his hair came in handy during the winter (he didn't have to wear the latest look in armor wear) and when his mother wished the floors washed she simply turned Reginald upside down, dipped his head into the old, oaken bucket and proceeded to cleans her home of filth and sin (two down-on-their-luck burlesque beauties).

But summer drove him mad

That's why King Zephyr threw him into the dungeon. There, lonely and languishing, Sir Reginald made a solemn oath to avenge himself on the despotic king the minute he was freed.

But he never was.

# MUTINY SCHWARTZ

Horribly offended by Capt. Bligh's now historic statement: "It's mutiny, Mr. Christian!" Mutiny, who was devoutly orthodox (he couldn't kill innocent Polynesians on the Sabbath), devised an ingenious method of revenge.

He converted all the crew and all the inhabitants of Tahiti to Hasidism and when he mutinied, he heard the incredulous scream of Capt. Bligh: "It's mutiny, Mr. Jewish?"

As those words were so shrilly uttered, Mutiny threw Bligh overboard and the whole crew cheered as Bligh was devoured by a ravenous gefilte fish.

# ZITCHIE POO

Zitchie was the famous Saville Row hairdresser. His styling was compared to art. And Art was compared to Queen Consort Camilla.

Poo, as his friends called him (his enemies called him "Bitchy Zitchie") first came to this country (from where, no one knows) as a poor immigrant (if he was rich he would've stayed put and been called Richie Zitchie Poo). And while trying to fit in and make it big, he made it smaller during a botched circumcision session.  Determined to overcome this rather harsh handicap, he hired himself out as a bargain basement gigolo and lost all his money in this mad cap adventure. It seemed that women wanted something a bit more tangible for their investment, and something a bit more.

Then, scraping together all he had, he opened his own hair dressing salon. His business was an overnight success and he turned his energies into bigger and better things.

He opened the world's largest beauty salon. From all over the world, large beauties would come to be Poo-Pooed (his trademarked look). Yet he would never divulge his secret ingredients (much like McDonald's but with warm buns). Which is why, one night, when Zitchie was alone in the salon, he was tortured by some competitive beauty saloners to give up his secret. Which he would not and did not do.

So you can only imagine what they did to poor Poo.

# THE END

Although the end of this book comes as no surprise to those of you who eventually expected to find it (and to those of you who longed for it earlier), you *will* be surprised to learn that this book has really been a lengthy dissertation on the mating habits of the South American bull frog.

# HANGNAIL HANK

Hangnail Hank didn't have a hangnail. He just loved to hang things on nails. Even himself.

He'd start with an extra-long, 6" nail, grab his happy hammer and smash that sucker into walls, trees, tires, whatever caught his fancy.

At one point, he climbed a ladder, drove a nail into the highest branch of a weeping willow, draped a rope around the nail, then his neck, then jumped.

Luckily, the rope wasn't well turned and Hank plummeted to the ground, breaking both his legs, his right arm, several ribs, his nose, the third finger of his left hand, and various and sundry organs inside which had, until this event, remained perfectly happy being left alone.

Upon his release from the hospital, Hank decided to forsake his hang nailing, or nail hanging, and chose a new and less-dangerous hobby:  stamp licking.

Unfortunately, this, too, proved undesirable because Hank's tongue, it seemed, served as a natural glue conductor and within his first few stamp licks, his tongue resembled nothing less than a philatelist's wet dream.

There are only a small handful of Royal Dukes in the realm (or Royal Dukes with small hands). And a footfull of plain, old ordinary dukes. One can give a finger to the handful and a kick to the footfull.

But in all the realm, there is only one Dook. The Dook of Shiteshire: Arthur Millstone Havingston Givingston was that first Dook. . He was most certainly not a royal duke. Or a royal flush. No, Arthur was simply the Dook of Shiteshire, one of the oldest titles in all the land.

It seems that when Melvin the Conqueror did what he did best, Arthur was right there beside him; or rather behind him because Arthur didn't want to get a boo-boo.

Since Arthur could not countenance the sight of blood, particularly his own, while Melvin was out chucking body parts here and there, Arthur was upchucking here and there.

In any event, upon saving Melvin's life when a deranged serf tried to kill him with a piece of straw (well, that's all he had), William, in gratitude, raised Arthur to the peerage. That way everyone could peer at Arthur and go: "Aw, that's not right. It was just a bleedin' piece of straw").

"But what's a Dook, Your Majesty?" asked Arthur.

"You don't know?" retorted Melvin.

"No, Sire."

"Excellent. We'll just keep it that way."

But upon entering the shire, Arthur, after long reflection, said to his squire: "Nothing happening here; let's go pillage over at Hampton."

Also, since Arthur was not looked upon kindly by the other nobles, he was routinely addressed as, "Your Graceless" and "Your Lowness".

Just imagine the pride Arthur took when he entered Westmonster and was announced as "His Lowness, the Dook of Shiteshire".

Being a dook, it was up to Arthur to foster a dynasty. So he chose as his wife Guinevere LaYum, a countess of Gascony; who brought untold riches and territory to the marriage (but since it was untold, we can't tell you about them).

Guinevere proved as fertile as the olive groves and produced fourteen children and seventeen tons of olives.

Guinevere and Arthur lived very happily until their happy Shiteshire was invaded by rampaging Vikings on a spring break.

Which was not a lucky break for Guinevere and Arthur.

However, their lineage has survived the eons and today the current Dook of Shiteshire sits in the House of Lords because, like his illustrious ancestor, no one can stand him.

Clarence Narrow was one of the greatest American legal minds of the eighteenth century. Which was a pity since he was living in the twentieth century.

Poor Clarence was never good at book learning and only passed the bar because he always passed the bar on his way home.

The problem was that because he really didn't grasp the basics of the law, he lost every case he ever tried. But he kept trying.

However, with a record of 0-324, nobody wanted to hire Clarence. Even for a simple jay walking offense. Or littering.

But then, when "Tetched Zeke" went to trial for that most foul and heinous crime that I need not repeat, the court appointed Clarence as his defense attorney. Clarence got right down to business.

He intently studied the evidence, interviewed all the witnesses, made sure that Zeke had an ironclad alibi and presented his defense to the jury, which took only five minutes to reach a decision.

'GUILTY!"

When the verdict was read, Clarence sat slumped in his chair muttering, "Well, I'll be hanged." But he wasn't.  Zeke was.

# THE LETTERS

Oh, Ms. Smith, I'd like you to send out a few of our standard new business letters.

To who, sir?

Well, there's the president of Acme Computers, Matthew Day.  The president of Ace Tire, Kevin Night.  The president of Standard Foods, Jamie Morrow. And the president of United Motors, Brett Gether.

So let me get this straight:  you want me to send letters out to Day, to Night, to Morrow, and to Gether.

Yes, but not at the same time. I don't want any conflicts.

So when do you want me to send them?

Well, I'd like you to send the letter to Day tonight, the one to Night tomorrow, the letter to Morrow today, and the one to Gether together with the one to Day.

OK. Let me get this straight:  you want me to send the letter to Day tomorrow, the letter to Night today, the one to Morrow tonight, and the one to Gether together with the one to Day.

No.  Please listen carefully.  I want the letter to Day tonight, the one to Night tomorrow, the letter to Morrow today, and the one to Gether together with the one to Day.

OK. So let me get this straight:  you want the letter to Gether tomorrow…

No, NO!  I want the letter to Day tonight, the one to Gether with the one to Day. Is that so difficult?

Well it wouldn't be if I could just get straight when you want the letter to Day, to Night, to Morrow and to Gether.

But I've told you three times already and it's quite simple:  I want the letter to Day tonight, the one to Night tomorrow, the letter to Morrow today, and the one to Gether together with the one to Day.

Sir, sir. I think I have it now. You want the letter to Day tonight, the one to Night tomorrow, the letter to Morrow today, and the one to Gether together with the one to Day.

That's it.

Well, now that I have the one to Day tonight, the one to Night tomorrow, the one to Morrow today and the one to Gether together with the one to Day, you can go to hell!

You've all heard the famous saying: "Early to bed, etc". Well, that was not from Pat.

Or "A penny saved, etc". Also, not from Pat.

No, Pat's platitudes took a more impenetrable turn.

For instance, here are just a few of Pat's more memorable utterings:

*One cannot tie two shoes at the same time.*

*Money is money. Honey is honey. And never the twain shall meet.*

*A heart attack is God's way of saying: "Hey, it could've been your Isle of Langerhans."*

*The seventh step will find you there.*

*You are not Humpty Dumpty.*

Yes, from the earliest age, Pat let these pearls fall trippingly from the tongue. Which was unfortunately forked. Like the devil. In fact, when it was time for Pat's christening, the minister ran shrieking into the Night and was never heard from again. Nor was the Night.

Be that as it may, nothing could stop Pat from spewing forth new and even more opaque platitudes:

*You only have one life. But ten toes.*

*The all-seeing eye hears all.*

*Why is not a bee an A?*

*Reach for the heavens and someone will try to tickle your underarm.*

*If an insect is outside, shouldn't it be an outsect?*

*A seat on a train makes you miss your stop.*

*A gentle admonition can be: Go to Helsinki.*

And just before Pat passed into eternity, owing to a severe bout of Clytemnestra, these were the last words whispered:

*Take the time to hear the flowers.*

This last, however, if followed by those suffering from hay fever, may lead to deafness.

"Oh, yes," he'd say jocularly, "it seems that I was destined to be a physician with a last name like that."

But he hid a deep, dark secret (who hides a shallow, light one?). His real last name was an old French noble name: DeCease. And who would want to be treated by a Dr. DeCease? Unless, of course, they already had a death wish.

(He was also abundantly silent about his first name).

So Dr. DeCease, or Doctor, went to specialize in the treatment of rare and exotic disorders of the mind.

He was the first to find a psychological cure for Nosa Nervosa; the affliction causing the sufferers to believe their noses were really hotdog buns. This would cause the sufferers to constantly try biting their noses while simultaneously grilling sausages.

He also pioneered procedures to lessen the effects of (and we use the correct Latin term here) Retro Ambulantes; the syndrome which doomed the sufferers to walk backwards. Especially in the armed services where soldiers are trained to march forward, Retro Ambulantes proved particularly problematic.

Finally, the breakthrough which earned Dr. Doctor the most prestigious of psychiatric awards, the much-coveted Medulla Oblongata Regatta Award, the cure for (Latin again) Dormiens In Caput – sleeping on one's head. Now, at first thought you might say how can anyone sleep on their heads? And you would be right. But try telling that to any Dormiens In Caput people you may encounter on your day to day.

# VINCENT VAN COUGH

Unlike Van Gogh who could paint with one ear, though his painting hand was steady, Vincent Van Cough had a different problem.

Every time he'd be ready to apply that one, last, incredibly beautiful brush stroke, he'd cough and the stroke would just about cause one.

Vincent tried everything. Holding his breath (he turned an indelible shade of Caribbean cobalt). Slurping double doses of Dr. Quack's Cough Elixir & Testosterone Combustor (this fostered a captivating onset of satyriasis which led to numerous morals charges but did nothing to cause a surcease of coughing). Breathing heavily into paper bags (though this is a grandmother's mythical cure for hiccups; in *this* instance, it proved the grandmother's myths to be true – of course Vincent did not have hiccups so the myth cannot be fairly judged thusly).

However, a miracle happened. During one of Vincent's more violent coughing fits, a famous French art critic, Antoine Pretentieux, passing by happened to hear the coughing and took the trouble to glance into the studio and was amazed at what he saw: a totally new artistic expression. It seemed that each time Vincent coughed and his brush stroke ran awry, it added an incendiary touch to his work. A look that the critic dubbed *Arta Inflammatoria.*

Suddenly, artists all over the world began coughing. And if they couldn't cough they'd push their brush hand with their other hand to try to achieve that special look that only Vincent could master.

Cough drop sales plummeted because everyone wanted to be seen as a true artist.

However, if Vincent couldn't cough he couldn't achieve that special look; so he had to make the toughest decision of his life:  remain an artistic master but endanger his lungs and his life, or take the new medicine to cure his cough and prolong his life; though he'd never be able to paint again.

He did as so many others had before him when faced with a seemingly insoluble dilemma: he climbed Mt. Blap, sat, and pondered. And while he sat and pondered he was pushed off Mt. Blap by the innumerable other people who'd reached the pinnacle and needed *their* space to sit and ponder. It wasn't very Zen, but it did solve the real estate problem that perennially afflicted Mt. Blap.

Penelope lived in New England in 1693. If the year doesn't ring a bell or elicit a light bulb to appear above your head, it was the height of the witch burnings.

So, evidently, Penelope, being brought up strict Puritan, knew the devil's handiwork when she saw it. And on market days his handiwork was usually in Stall 666, exhibiting lovely, embroidery with flowers and birds.

Penelope was so fastidious in her demeanor and décor that she would not permit any male of the species to even touch her hand. Her foot was another matter. Any boy could touch her foot if he so desired, and for some special boys, Penelope would remove her shoe.

'IT'S THE DEVIL'S DOING", shouted Patience Zebulon, the head Sunday school mistress (she was also the reverend Josiah Bible's mistress, but that's another story).

"YES! YES!", retorted the usual mob gathering; nothing better to do than stand around throwing stones at poor Penelope, hopping up and down, one foot then the other, and rubbing sticks together to create a flame.

However, on this particular Sunday, the heavens opened and the most severe rain storm since Noah inundated the iniquitous little hamlet.

Penelope, seeing her chance to escape, did so.

Once the rain stopped, the villagers, headed by Josiah Bible, lit a torch and screamed for the people to follow him (which was silly since it was noon and there was no need for a torch).

Into the dark, foreboding woods the Puritans scampered, shouting for Penelope and singing praises that more of their Puritan pretties had not been so accursed. Yet, unbeknownst to the mob, Penelope had sought and found shelter in the rickety hut of Humanity Dove, a rickety septuagenarian hag once burned at the steak but only rare.

"It's lucky ya found yer way here, girly", said Humanity.

"Yes, yes, it truly is", answered Penelope.

"What did ya do, lass? Couple with a goat? Have blintzes?"

"Oh, no, mistress. I permitted a boy, well several, to touch my unshod foot."

"Pshaw, that ain't nothing'. In my day ya had t' couple with a goat, or at least the parson, t' warrant a burnin'."

"Oh, no, I wasn't to be burned. Just stoned."

"Ah, nothing's nothing'. Ya need a good fire lit underya t' know what real retribution tastes like."

"Well, please begging your pardon, mistress, but the mob has passed and I think I'll be on my way. I thank you for your kindness in secreting me for a spell."

"Spell? Did ya say spell?"

And with that, Humanity turned Penelope into a goat.

# MARVIN SHTUP

If you've heard of The Academy Awards, then Marvin Shtup will never be mentioned in the same sentence.

You see, Marvin Shtup's life ambition was to name motion pictures; and he did, but just falling short of the titles that have become classics. For instance:

GONE WITH THE BREEZE

BEN HIM

THE NINE COMMANDMENTS

THE MALTESE PARROT

QUEEN KONG

SOME LIKE IT WARM

DR. YES

BONNIE AND CLAUDE

THE FIANCE OF FRANKENSTEIN

THE KING'S TALK

APOLOYPSE SOON

THE GODPAPPA

FIDDLER ON THE VERANDAH

THE GOOD GATSBY

And the list goes on. And on.

And though Marvin's titles always missed the mark, yours can, too. Just come up with titles that fall short. Make a game of it. Let's see how miserably you do. Put Marvin to shame. Call your group Marvin's Minions". Or some such erroneous assemblage.

# SHERLOCH HOMES

In late Victorian London, the seat of the greatest empire the world had ever known, criminal activity was rampant and, it seemed, unstoppable.

There were the Sneaky Blunders Bunch, the Chinese Chopstick Chaps, the Calcutta Curry Crazies, and perhaps the most sinister of all, the Loch Ness Nuisances.

Scotland Yard seemed incapable of dealing with these gangs (although they had a regular poker game going with them every Wednesday night) and it is said that Queen Victoria herself was not amused.

But then, out of the thick-as-cement fog one night, a lone, tall, slender figure emerged at the corner of Piccadilly and Punchandjudy. His name was Sherloch Homes (though he nor his family had any connection whatsoever with kilts).

Homes. A name that would come to strike terror in the hearts (and kidneys) of the London underworld (the London overworld was also populated by criminals, but of a different nature). No, they were not terrified of the man, just the name.

Why, many was the time the constabulary would hear various and sundry felons shriek in terror: "Homes? Homes? No! No!  Please keep that name away from me! For love of God, no! No!"

No one could understand why Homes caused such consternation among the criminal class, including Homes. Because Sherloch  Homes was nothing more than a local milk deliveryman.

Homes, a hypochondriac at heart, would call on his physician, Dr. Whatsin, and, from time to time, would permit the good doctor to hop aboard his milk wagon and go for a merry spin around town.

However, there was danger lurking around every turn (it generally doesn't lurk straight ahead) and one early morning when Homes and Whatsin were delivering milk to an especially appreciative Cockney housewife, tragedy struck.

The Loch Ness Nuisances had been lying in wait (well, not actually lying, perhaps squatting would be more precise) and they pounced (well, not actually pounced because how many times have you ever seen anyone or anything pounce; it was more like seized upon) Homes and Whatsin, stole the milk and ran off with the wagon.

Homes and Whatsin immediately reported the incident to Scotland Yard, but since the attackers were Loch Ness Nuisances, Scotland Yard harkened to their heritage and had no interest in capturing the culprits.

To this day, the Loch Ness Nuisances continue their evil ways. But there is absolutely no truth to the rumor that they own the very successful restaurant chain, Bagels & Lochs.

Sebastian had a singularly unique occupation. He was an aardvark whisperer.

Yes, there is a famous dog whisperer and horse whisperer, but none had the solitary station that Sebastian occupied.

It was odd that Seb (as he liked to be addressed), who lived in the Aleutian Islands, nowhere near any aardvarks, nor most any other like faunae, would achieve such distinguished heights.

While studying ice formations in a sub-Sahara African university (an odd choice to study since there was no ice to be seen, except in various and sundry libations)
an aardvark happened to startle Seb while sleeping (Seb, not the aardvark).

The aardvark bared his ferociously sharp fangs and Seb whispered (while simultaneously irrigating his pants), "Calm down, paly, just let me get back to sleep."  With that, the aardvark did precisely as directed, let Seb continue his slumber, but waited patiently for Seb to awaken. And when he did awake, the aardvark began doing tricks.

He sat up. He played dead. He rolled over. He fetched. And all without Seb having to say one word. Yes, Seb knew immediately what his life's calling would be.

He named the aardvark Adam (see the significance?) and without the aid of a leash, they began their trek across South Africa. During their travels, Seb whispered to innumerable aardvarks who

responded to Seb much as Adam had done. In fact, by the time Seb reached the most southern tip of South Africa, there were approximately 23,262 aardvarks following him.

Obviously, this put a strain on the native aardvark population and Seb was forced to bid adieu to his aardvark hordes by whispering them to go home. With tears in their eyes, they turned north and returned from whence they came.

Now it was time to return to the Aleutians and Seb had to decide what would be best for Adam; accompany Seb to the Aleutians or return to his family.

Seb, though it would piece his heart after all he and Adam had been through, whispered that it would be best if Adam returned home

Adam cried and pleaded to stay with Seb, but when Seb was adamant that Adam return home, Adam bit him, which resulted in Seb's instantaneous demise. At that point Adam screamed: "WHISPER! HA!"

# SHVESTEH ESTHER

For those of you not entirely conversant with the Yiddish language. "shvesteh" is the Yiddish word for sister. So, in essence, we'll be speaking of Sister Esther.

Now, Sister Esther doesn't sound like a likely name for a nun; we expect Sister Mary Margaret, or Sister Margaret Mary, etc. However, Pope Loquacious XII himself placed Esther with the Sisterhood (Robin Hood wasn't available).

Shvesteh Esther began her life in the tiny Polish shtetel of Oy Gevalt, a tad north of the tiny Polish shtetel of Shweig Shayne. Her father, Shmendrick, was the town crier (anybody with a sad story would impart the tale to Shmendrick and he would cry till the cows came home, which wasn't often because no one in the shtetel owned any cows; or chickens for that matter; though they did have a plethora of adorable vermin).

Shvesteh's mother, Meiskite, had been Miss Shtetel of 1253 and was living on her laurels (a house or shack would've been preferable, but you know those Miss Shtetels).

The funny thing about her family, the Bullvons, was that they were not Jewish. They had Jewish names, they lived in a Jewish shtetel, they kept a kosher home, they liked Charlton Heston, but they were, in reality, Druids. And many's the time people would say to them, "Funny, you don't look Druish."

# FORGOTTEN ROMAN EMPERORS

Thanks to various and sundry movies and television programs, we all know the names of Augustus, Nero, and most damnable of all, Caligula.

However, there are several Roman emperors that history has chosen to overlook. Or completely forget. Here are just a few:

**Marcus Ridiculous**:  A complete moron raised to the imperial purple as a Praetorian Guard practical joke. They killed him after the joke wore off.

**Tulius Hilarious**:  When you hear about playing the palace, he not only played the palace, but built it and forced the patricians to listen to his stand up for hours on end. The Praetorian Guard did not find him funny and killed him.

**Lucius Verbotious**:  Lucius loved to talk. And talk. And talk. About everything and absolutely nothing. The Praetorian Guard killed him just to shut him up.

**Decimus Disastrous**:  One of the worst emperors in that he thought himself a great general and led three legions into total decimation by the Germanic barbarians. The Praetorian Gard didn't have the chance to kill him. The barbarians did.

**Sublius Suspicious**: He didn't trust everyone and thought everyone was out to kill him. He was right. The Praetorian Guard did.

**Publius Odious**: Everyone hated Odious. Especially the Praetorian Guard. So…

**Faustus Fastidious**: Everything had to be just so. Scabbards polished, tunics trim, swords sharp, helmets glistening. If you had a speck of lint on your breastplate,  you'd be thrown to the lions in the Colosseum.  Guess where he wound up?

**Gnaeus Cantankerous**: He was a pain in the neck so the Praetorians obliged.

**Julius Abstemious**: Because he didn't drink, he wouldn't permit anyone else to do so. No wine in the palace. So very soon no Abstemious in the palace.

**Catalus Venomous**: Need we say more?

Senator Horace Flibidibidgit came from a long, lustrous line of Flibidibidgits.

There was the Hon. Josiah Flibidibidgit, the county dog catcher who many believed to be more at ease chasing bitches.

There was Gen. Slocum Flibidibidgit, the infamous rebel general at Gettysburg who decided to charge to the rear during Picket's famous charge to the Union front.

And who could forget the doomed astronaut Ebeneezer Flibidigibit who lost track of time when due back at the launch pad and is still up there, somewhere, on the moon?

Yes, Horace had much to be proud of. Which is why he ran for the Senate (he also ran for the bus but the driver wouldn't wait).

Horace launched his campaign in his home town of Feh, Arkansas and all the Flibidigibits showed up. Those who were not incarcerated, or missing, or hiding in another country without extradition arrangements. In short, two people showed up. But since Feh didn't have many people who could vote, or read, or write, or who knew which century this was, Horace did wonderfully well.

Then Horace had the other thrilling debate with his candidate, Cincinnati Slim, an inveterate gambler who had never been anywhere near Cincinnati and at four hundred and seventy two pounds was nowhere near slim.

Horace easily won the debate because Slim never spoke; he just kept munching on dried lobster claws and cottage cheese.

Once in the Senate, Horace was assigned to the highly unimportant No Way and Moans committee; and he would've served admirably had he not got lost in the Senate underground tram tunnels. He didn't want to ask for directions for fear of being a laughing stock by the other party and being ostracized for gross stupidity by his own.

So there he remains, somewhere deep in the bowels of the Senate. And looking at the Senators, we can only imagine what those bowels are like.

As her name implies, Sympathy had that for everything.

She was empathetic to toad stools, tin foil, foie gras, rubber bands, finger nails, watch bands, bubbles, ink and the list goes on.

Notice the word "everything". Because while Sympathy had true empathy for things, she lacked the same exuberant passion for people.

Needless to say this was a major drawback at Nobel Peace Prize time.

However, you may have missed it, but there is no mention above of her overriding sympathy for animals.

She empathized with bats' ears, raccoon placentas, kangaroo pouches, cheetah teeth, jackal tails, otter udders, Tasmanian Devil snouts, clown fish makeup, octopus pusses, and bunny biceps.

This still did not win any points with the Nobel Prize Judging board.

So she took another route. She feigned sympathy for automobile parts. Still nothing. Major box office disasters? Nope. TV reality shows? (What do you think?). And, finally, retail stores' bargain basements. Over and out.

When last seen Sympathy was petting a prone piranha.

Merrily was the first female trolley conductor in Little Stink, Michigan.

There'd been a long history of male conductors but Merrily broke new ground. That's because she also used a jackhammer as a road builder.

In fact, Merrily had the honor of not only conducting the trolleys in Little Stink, but in many cases, building the very roads the trolleys rode on.

Now some may say that's a conflict of interest, but since she had no interest in conflict, the charge is spurious.

Merrily conducted the trolley from 1903 to 1908 when Little Stink suffered not only an earthquake, but a hurricane, a tornado, and a flood all at the same time. It also suffered from a lack of prevention, so Little Stink, in reality, became Tiny Stink; a name approved by the Michigan legislature.

However, the good people of Tiny Stink (and some of the bad people, too) chipped in, put their shoulders to the wheel (when they could find a wheel) and rebuilt the town back to its former glory as Little Stink, the pride of the Upper Peninsula.

So what did Merrily do during and after the disasters? Well, during the earthquake, she stood with shakers attached to her body filled with ice cream and syrup to make the first Quake Shakes (which we enjoy to this day).

During the tornado, she met a girl named Dorothy with her dog, Toto, and directed them to safety somewhere over the rainbow.

During the flood she started the Little Stink Yacht Club but it didn't stay afloat. And during the hurricane, she attached pretty paper cutouts to prison windows so the paper flapping against the cell bars would create the feeling of angel wings for the inmates. Something to lift their spirits. But it was a devil of a time getting most to believe in angels.

After the above disasters, Merrily was promoted to Trolley In Transit Supervisor (TITS) and kept all the trolleys on the right track. Pity the same can't be said for Merrily.

www.ingramcontent.com/pod-product-compliance
Lightning Source LLC
Chambersburg PA
CBHW040953050726

47507CB00024B/403